good deed rain

Credits

Cover design: Michael Paulus

Cover photo: Allen Frost

Back cover photo: Rustle Frost

Illustrations: Allen Frost

Apple by TFK!

Thank you to Larry Smith
and Bottom Dog Press

If you have enjoyed this book
please share it with someone

ACROSS THE STREET FROM THE HOLY SAINT

AND *Lemonade*

WRITING AND ILLUSTRATIONS
BY ALLEN FROST

written on Franklin Street

INTRODUCTIONS:

Across the Street from the Holy Saint was completed November 24, 2000 at our second Bellingham rental house, on Franklin Street. It was a big step up from our first Dracula-crypt house at Grant Street. Now we had a willow tree in our yard. There was a path made of broken white marble slabs leading up to the porch. I started this book when we noticed our neighbor's resemblance to a Hollywood comedy legend. What a story! Stop the Press! Another great thing about that house—at night you could look through the dark willow leaves and see the Herald sign glowing.

Lemonade is a little book I finished in February 2003. You'll notice it features William Carlos Williams' red wheelbarrow. *Lemonade* was also written on Franklin Street.

Allen Frost
October 31, 2013
Bellingham, Washington

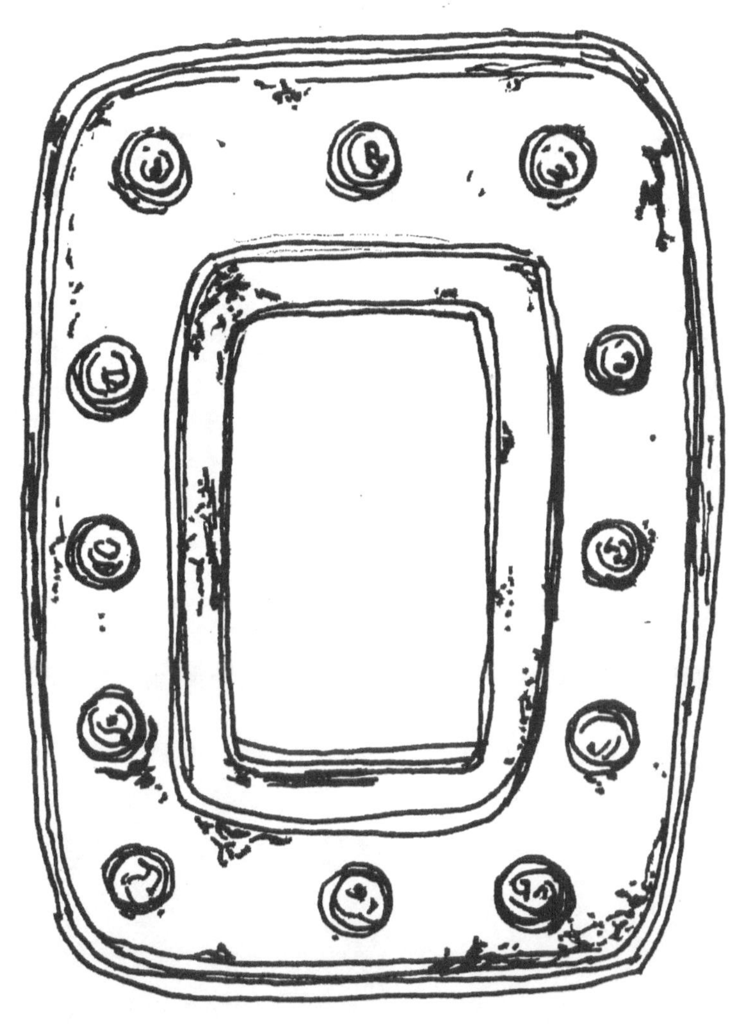

ACROSS the STREET from the HOLY SAINT

WATCHING
STAR-STRUCK
IN ANOTHER FIFTY YEARS
A SONG
REPAIRS
LOOK
THE KING
THE STORY OF ALBERT
IN ONE STEP
IMAGINATION
SHOPPING
THE SOUND
BUG
SPECTACLE
THE NEW FENCE
THE OLD FENCE
A HALO IN MY HOUSE
LAUREL & HARDY
THE NAMES OF RIVERS
FAMILIAR
THE CRIB
COFFEE AND TEA LEAVES
A STEEL LETTER O
VENICE
PAT HATTER'S CAR
CLOUDY AND QUIET
MURMURING
THIS MORNING
ELECTRICITY
NEVERMIND

Meanwhile Captain Jack had returned to his cave where
he sat gravely mapping out his plans for the coming battle.

Captain Jack, Modoc Renegade
by Doris Palmer Payne

When I got home I spent quite some time with a mirror,
but I couldn't figure it. I took to worrying about the thing.
I began taking a deeper interest in the doings of Bing
Crosby and I started talking about him whenever I was
around the Broadway know-it-alls. Little by little I
acquired anecdotes about Crosby, and after two or three
months the fact dawned on me: if I hadn't been a Crosby
man before, I was a Crosby man now.

Life In A Putty Knife Factory
by H. Allen Smith

"I grew up loving Laurel and Hardy."

Albert Brooks, 1997

1. *WATCHING*

Albert Jacks has just found out he is going to have triplets. Everything happening in his life led to this miracle. And who knows what will happen after they are born? It's waiting to be seen.

I don't want it to sound like I spend all my time watching over him, but whenever I can, I watch Albert from my porch or from around a window curtain inside. I see the world as a patchwork of movies, with the star Albert Jacks drifting in and out of my life.

2. *STAR-STRUCK*

Before this continues any further, I should explain that Albert Jacks, of course, is the name of the famous Californian comedian/film director. I discovered my neighbor's uncanny resemblance one day out of the blue, and that was when the star-struck fascination took hold of my life.

I guess part of it too is that nobody else seems to be aware. Other people live around him, park their tired cars on the street next to his, mow their lawns beside his house and nod at him yet don't even know the truth.

The first thing I did was go to the movie store and rent all of Albert Jacks' films to study them very carefully. I discovered, sure enough, it had to be true: for whatever reason, Albert had moved anonymously from sunny L.A to the mostly rainy world just south of Canada's border.

3. *IN ANOTHER FIFTY YEARS*

I had to get ready for work. The cuckoo clock over by the icebox just hopped out to remind me. It's one o'clock.

I picked up the birdcage I bring with me to work. It's filled with little paint tubes, small cans and a milky jar of thinner. There are more than twenty brushes in the pockets of my white dress. I feel like a bird with all these painted feathers.

The front door closed with the heavy clang of Tibetan bells strung inside. What a beautiful day! A bright early October blue sky, the sting of the sun on my face, sharp, cold with winter starting in. It felt good.

All around, there are peaks of houses with black electric wires drawn over them like puppet strings. The factory beyond shook out a white and rusty cloud. Dropping around it is a frame of leaves from my willow tree on the left side of the yard, with the fantastic old wooden church growing into a spire next door.

And there, right across the street is Albert's house. It looks like it could make a great haunted house in another fifty years.

I walked on the cracked marble path towards it.

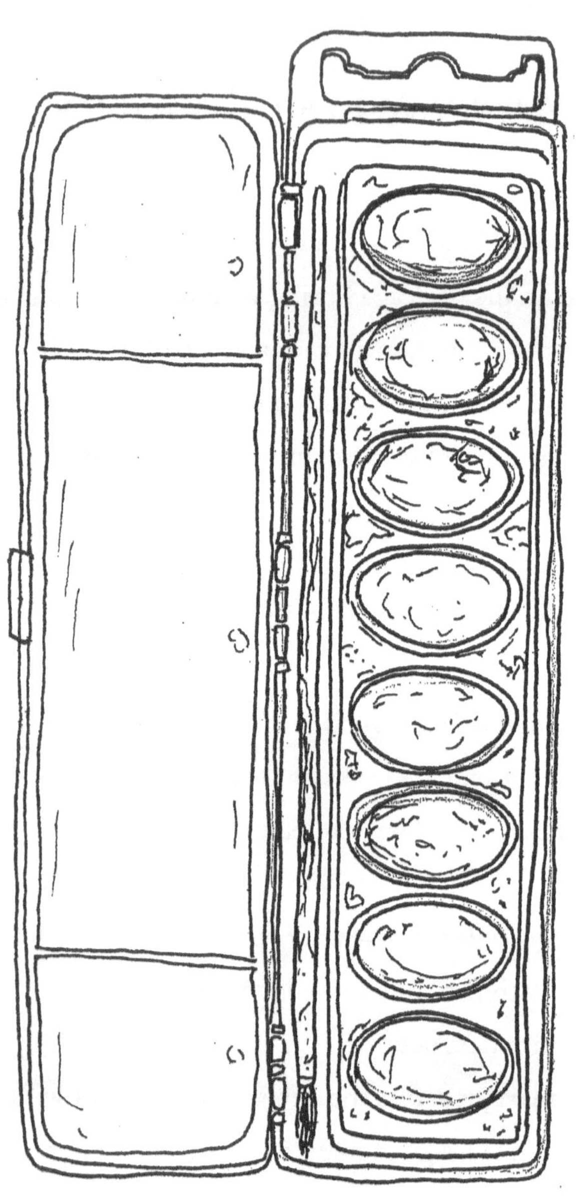

weathered clues

4. A SONG

I finished a song in my head. I love walking around this neighborhood of old houses. Mostly I walk down the alleys beside the paint worn wood and blackberry thorns, but I skipped the last alley. There's a dog in there, chained from a porch, and he frazzles at anything passing near.

I swung the paint birdcage in my hand as I walked. Once by accident on this same route, I left a green Grimm's fairytale trail of color all the way home. Yet after all this time and weather, only a few places exist where you can still find them. They are small weathered clues of paint only Sherlock Holmes would know.

5. *REPAIRS*

Long ago, stars were painted on landmarks around the city. It's my job to touch them up now and then, to keep them shining bright. I'm not the only one to do this work. There's been a long line of people before me, and there will be more when I'm gone.

Underneath a bridge where the highway drove overhead on steel girders, pigeons and cement, I worked on the color orange. Between red and yellow, I covered a hopeless word someone wrote. They write those sometimes. A little more orange and it will be gone.

The loud avenue roared behind me while I finished painting the wall, until the star looked new. Whenever I need to, I do these repairs; it's the work of some Greek mythology the way I have to keep at it.

And there are still more places around town that I may need to repaint today.

6. *LOOK*

I chose this last bridge because it tunnels through the quiet end of the park. It's a peaceful place to finish a day's work. It's rare that it ever gets written on, but I like to keep it glowing with fresh paint. Sometimes people walk by, look, and say hello or compliment me. I've even found flowers waiting for me on the sidewalk.

When I'm done, I carry the birdcage to a favorite spot in the Japanese maples, to a cedar bench where I rest. In the pool next to me, goldfish submarine among the umbrella lotus leaves.

7. *THE KING*

The King's car is planted somewhere below the park in blackberry vines, on a road that turns into dirt, mud and gravel. He has his job too. He's the King of this park, watching over it and caring for it.

Over the lawns and city forest sheltering him, I rustle off the slope, out of fallen leaves onto the royal road. I see his gray rusty car slanted off into the shoulder of that maple grove where it's been parked for some years now.

8. *THE STORY OF ALBERT*

The King was sitting on the hood counting his thoughts. His eyes were closed. He could have been asleep.

I almost left him that way, but then his eyes opened. "There you are," he said. It was like he was waiting for me.

Reaching into his sweater, he pulled out some flowers, clovers that grew around the wheels of his car. Each season the wild flowers change from lilacs to daisies, to dandelions. Each color too comes and goes, in blues, whites, reds and yellows. "These are for your hair," he said and laced them gently while his caterpillar-slow words thanked me for my work on the stars. I keep the kingdom beautiful and he pays me in flowers.

I smiled and would have stayed for a while, but I was eager to get back to the story of Albert.

on the porch

9. *IN ONE STEP*

There are so many trees around my house I can walk from the sunny path into cold shade in one step. A little table in the yard under the willow becomes a shrine among the trees. I keep books propped open, candles, leaves, berries, and flowers spread all over. I have tied the willow branches with strings of plastic jewels, chimes, beads and necklaces.

I sat down in a chair on the porch. There's a guitar hanging on the wall. I keep it fed with sunflower seeds, hoping birds will come to nest in it. I don't know what's taking them.

Albert's car was gone, off to his job at the Herald. The house was quiet. Maybe his wife was in there, I didn't know. She doesn't seem to come out anymore. Last summer she was out everyday stirring her herb garden. Once she brought me some sage. I still have it on a windowsill. It reaches over a dry little circus of pale orange ladybug shells.

10. *IMAGINATION*

A rainbow of light crept along a cobweb. The spider sat there resting as Albert's brown car drove into leafy view. Wearing sunglasses and a blue T-shirt from the KGUS radio station, he moved quickly from his car, through the gate of his fence, up the straight short path to the door of his green three story house. The door opened then shut behind him.

I couldn't hear what was happening on the other side of their walls and windows. They stayed dark, reflecting the neighborhood. I sat back in my chair and closed my eyes and my imagination showed me Albert.

There is a stairway near the door. His wife is in a room upstairs, lying in a bed and holding a book on her stomach, the warm roof for her three babies. Albert asks her how she feels. He sits on the edge of the bed and listens. He tells her about his day at the newspaper building. She runs her hands over her belly. Albert remembers. She brightens when he opens a paper bag and takes out a Chinese dinner.

11. *SHOPPING*

I do my shopping with the Russians and the other poor. We come here because this place is old and the prices hover no more than a dollar for most things.

I guess I can blame Albert for my Chinese food craving. I headed for the frozen glass doors at the end of the room.

The *Mr. Lees* brand, covered with white ice and dragons, is the best. There are several different flavors. I reached for the red one.

Some hands back in the steam were piling bags of vegetables tightly towards the glass. What if they caught me and dragged me into a Siberian gulag? Before I could see it come true, I closed the door in a hurry. It fogged over with snow.

12. *THE SOUND*

Walking back up the hill, a block from the store, I could feel something was wrong. My quiet, beautiful neighborhood trembled with the roar of some machine. It got louder as I neared home and the sound took form.

A small yellow bulldozer grumbled on the lawn in front of Albert's house. It clawed the ground like a bull, letting go with a black cloud, then it went running and hit into the garden fence. And Albert was driving the thing!

Why was he ripping holes in their land? What of that poor lady full of life in there, holding her belly? Had the whole world gone crazy and dangerous? I couldn't think straight, it felt like a war. I crept along the roots of the hedges on my side of the street.

13. *BUG*

I couldn't make it any further than the next maple tree. That's where I had to stop and hold onto the elephant leg of it for a while.

Albert had finished knocking down his fence with a few brutal crashes of the bulldozer. He steered the thing as it ripped into gears like a bug. Miraculously, the gateway managed to remain. The row of climbing roses clung to it like Titanic survivors.

Albert tried to back the yellow machine onto the trailer behind his car. He missed the ramp though. You could easily imagine this as a scene in one of his comedies. On the second jerky try he got the bulldozer onto the trailer and stopped just short of driving it off the end into his car.

He took off his sunglasses and rubbed his forehead with the radio station T-shirt, showing his stomach.

"Oh!" I cried. Suddenly it occurred to me—maybe he's in the middle of making a movie!

14. *SPECTACLE*

Albert turned the motor off and went on without stopping for a take. It was the sort of thing Orson Welles would direct.

Albert jumped back to the pavement, walked over to kick the fence boards which splintered over his garden. Beside him in the grass was a new looking wheelbarrow. It held a silver shovel.

Quiet, real life seemed to prevail. I couldn't hear my footsteps as I traveled back home under the flickering effects of sky, trees, and this latest spectacle in Albert Jacks' next movie.

15. *THE NEW FENCE*

The heavy black velvet curtain I hide behind was tied open with reedy branches from my willow tree.

The raking sounds of scraping leaves from across the street scratched away as Albert stuffed the remains of his fence into bags.

I heard Albert call to his wife, "Don't worry. We'll get more plants. I'll fill it with new flowers." Albert picked around the debris and kicked a board, promising, "The new fence will be much better."

16. *THE OLD FENCE*

Still, I felt, why did it have to happen? I liked the old fence. It may have dipped in a spot or two, but I was used to that. Their herbs and berries grew so pleasantly beside it. What a shame…What kind of a comedy movie was this?

I went into the corner of my room where I kept matches on the bookshelf. I lit the candles on the wall. Their yellow glow and shadows calmed me. I sat back into the red easy-chair that seemed two centuries old by now.

I reached a hand towards the walnut colored radio. If only it could play its first memories. That would be something beautiful, to listen to a day in 1932.

17. *A HALO IN MY HOUSE*

In the back yard, I gathered some of last summer's vegetables. I stepped around the planted statues until I had found enough to eat. The kitchen steamed out the window like a kettle.

With a handful of cabbage leaf and some squash, I returned inside. Enough candles glowed to make a halo in my house.

As I closed the window curtains in the front room, the only thing I noticed about Albert's house was all the bags full of fence and chopped flower stems sitting on the sidewalk like teabags.

I wondered about my old film projector and the cardboard shoebox full of Super-8 films. It's been so long since I thought of them. It feels like I dreamed them.

After I put a pan of water on to steam, I went looking.

18. *LAUREL & HARDY*

The King gave me this box a long time ago. I leave it under the stacks of records, paints and photographs. It was heavy to bear into the kitchen, onto the table.

I took out the funny looking projector. You don't see them much anymore. It's made of blue plastic and metal. It clicks out two arms to hold the hoops that roll the film. When plugged in, the electricity purrs and pours out a light of moving pictures on the wall.

I looked inside the box again. Films are kept in there in small boxes painted with Laurel & Hardy, Charlie Chaplin, Laurel & Hardy, Abbott & Costello, Buster Keaton, and more Laurel & Hardy. I've seen them all before but I keep going back to them. They are maps to other worlds. Even when I sleep their memory runs into my dreams like rivers.

19. *THE NAMES OF RIVERS*

The Gold Rush

That's My Wife

Have Badge, Will Chase

One Week

Wrong Again

The Circus

From Soup to Nuts

The Gold Rush

Three Ages

20. *FAMILIAR*

My attention stayed on movies, my ritual for the night. I waited until the sun went down, when the back of the land was a sharp line of black roofs and trees, when the red neon light spelling HERALD went on.

I felt like I could never tire of these familiar eight films. Putting them in the spindle works of the projector, the clicking whir brought the long-ago comedians back to life.

21. *THE CRIB*

The Crib, the title card read.

The black space in between was flecked with white snow and scratches.

With Albert Jacks, the words went on. I stared at the wall as the film magically began.

Albert fit right into the 1920's world, stopping a black steaming jalopy in front of a furniture store. He ran around the back of the car, jumped in the air as it backfired, and hurried up to the automobile door to help out his pregnant wife.

Inside the store a gigantic man was waiting for them. On the tops of his eyes were painted thick eyebrows, heavy as vulture wings. He flapped his arms at a row of baby cribs.

Albert looked at them quickly. They were like little painted boats. The salesman pointed at one. Albert shook his head, held up his arms wide and counted one, two, three fingers.

The shop owner staggered backwards with his hands to his face.

Just then, the film ran through the projector, returning the wall to white light.

22. COFFEE AND TEA LEAVES

On the way downtown I stopped for a cup of coffee at the café. I went to the garden in the back and rested on a wooden chair near the holly tree. Birds hopped in the yellow and green tops of trees.

Had I really seen Albert Jacks in one of my movies last night? I was sort of afraid to look through the films again. It seemed as though I put the roll back in a Laurel & Hardy box before I went to bed. Maybe I only dreamed it.

My fingers warmed around the steaming clay cup. A black flight of crows travelled by, like tea leaves in the sky.

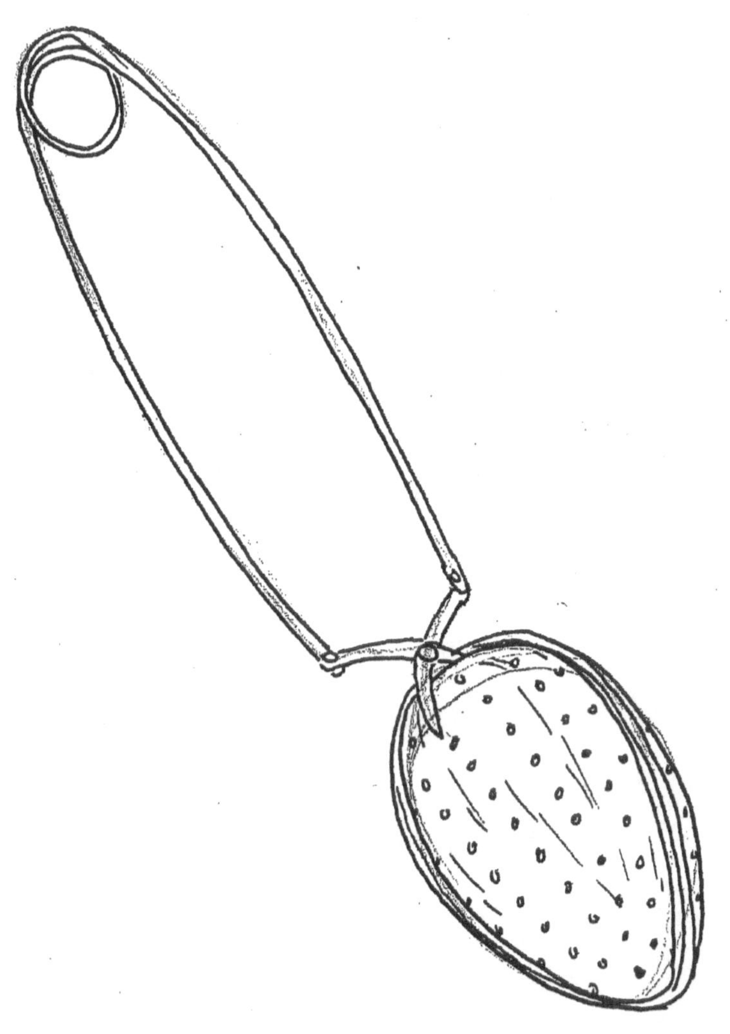

for a cup

the sloping alley

23. *A STEEL LETTER O*

Down the sloping alley I had a good view of the *Herald* newspaper building. Once a week at this late morning time, I visit a friend of mine and here I was again, stopped at his garage door.

Blue and white shocks of welding light showed between the hinges and gaps. After waiting until it was silent for a moment, I gave the secret knock on the chipped wood.

The door had a grate in it like a speakeasy. It slid open and goggled eyes stared at me. "Oh! Come on in."

The locks released and let me inside. Set upright in the middle of the garage was a steel, ten foot tall letter O. Pat had been working on it for a couple months, and it finally looked done.

"I just wanted to see how you are," I told Pat Hatter. He clung to the welding torch as he crossed to the wall.

"Watch this," he said and turned off the lights. When he clicked another switch on, the giant letter burned in the middle of the room like a red furnace.

24. *VENICE*

Taking the alleys back home, I thought of Venice while I paddled through those narrow canals. On either side of me, piles of ivy covered old cars that were sinking in. Everything was a part of a worn-out make-believe.

I rested on a ledge and stretched my legs in front of me. Some orange leaves rattled on the gray tar in the wind. They rustled and clowned and tumbled over each other whenever the wind brought them to life. Then they would stop and wait for life again.

25. *PAT HATTER'S CAR*

Pat Hatter's car went by me. It was speckled with green dots. Somehow he didn't see me as he flew by. His mind probably on making giant letters glow in the dark.

After his sudden appearance and disappearance, I got to my feet, and went back to my walk, through the dark trees and the old wooden alleys warped and brooding from all the rain.

26. *CLOUDY AND QUIET*

The fence bags were gone from Albert's lawn, but in their place stood a huge cardboard box. Whatever was in it had been removed. The flaps were left open at the top. Crunched packing snow was scattered out in little bits onto the grass and cement. Although I couldn't read the lettering on its side from my porch, I was sure the box held something for the triplets.

Was it a big crib? How strange that it arrived only a day after Albert Jacks' film previewed on my wall! I wondered what would happen if I ran the film projector again? More predictions? Or would it be Laurel & Hardy?

Anyway, I had been outside long enough for the sun to dip. It was cloudy and quiet and time to go inside.

the box held something

27. MURMURING

The willow tree was tuned like an antenna to the first drops of rain and wind. The drapes shifted beside the window as I creaked the corner chair springs. I was listening to the neighborhood with its sounds of an occasional car driving past, a bird singing, a closing door. Minute by minute the weather was changing. Day was turning into night. A dark blanket was being pulled over.

Looking at the Philco radio, I thought of the people from that time listening when the golden dial used to buzz into life. It shined with the sound of Jack Benny, The Phil Harris Show, Bob Hope, The Shadow, Boston Blackie, Our Miss Brooks, The Whistler, Bing Crosby. Those far away people are captured in there, murmuring in radio air, alive in the invisible land pictured in your mind.

28. *THIS MORNING*

Thinking talked me to sleep. A dream was lost in there where I don't remember. When I woke up, I heard rain brushing all over the house, then came a sharp knocking at the door.

Oh, I forgot! The Social Health officer was coming this morning! Now I remembered.

Jumping up, I put on a long brown robe. I could see his blur on the window curtain, waiting for me to open the door.

The officer took over the porch with an octopus of equipment. There were big suitcases, tubes and plastic robot-looking parts. He was soaked from the rain, going back and forth on the marble walk from his white van to my house.

29. ELECTRICITY

"That tree in your yard is very…interesting," he said.

"Thank you." I was sure that my decorated willow would end up in his notes later.

He worked all the equipment in from the wet porch, stacking it in my living room like a wall.

Pointing at the candles on the ledges and bookshelves, he asked me, "You still have electricity don't you?"

I nodded.

"Without it I won't be able to tell you anything." He closed the door and roped a thick black cable over to the socket. Plugging it in caused the room to shimmer for a moment. All the machinery blinked fiercely and hummed at high pitch. He raised his voice, "If you will bring a chair over here, we can get started."

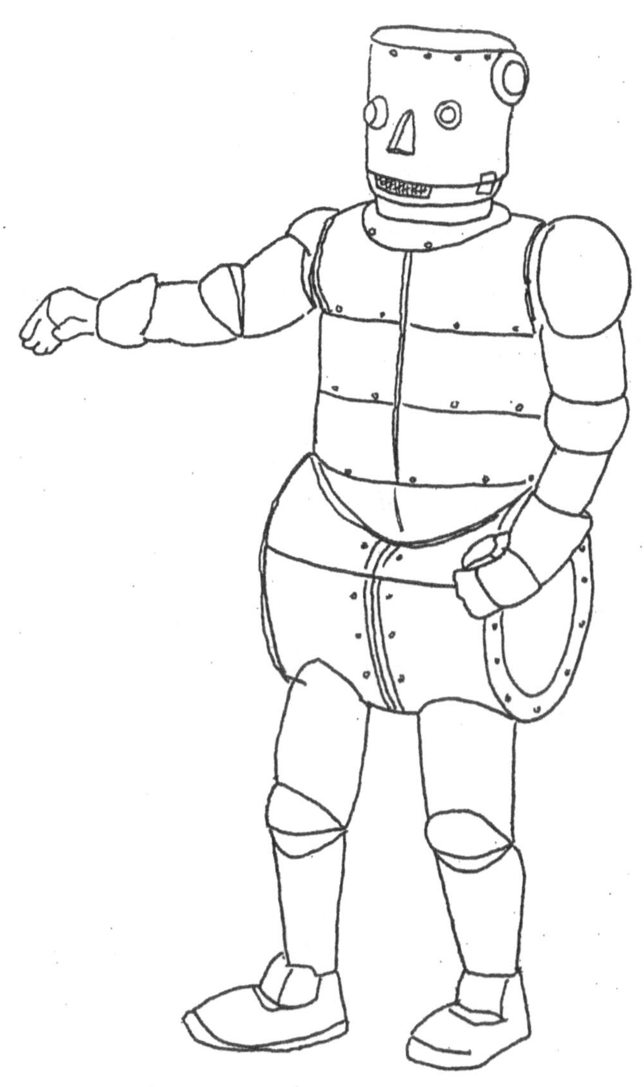

machinery blinked fiercely

30. *NEVERMIND*

It took him another half an hour or so to hook all the gadgets and gizmos onto me. I could barely move from the weight of wires and tubes and cables attaching me to his machines. How could this jumble of mad science possibly tell anything about me? But every time it ran electricity through me, it spelled out something on its computer screen.

Nevermind. I just let it happen. I listened through its clatter to the peaceful shower of rain, out to car wheels sluicing up and down the rivers running on top of the road. Meditating, catching every last bit of weather, swirled the willow tree, holding out leaves to comfort me. I closed my eyes and went deeper. This would all be over soon.

31. *DR. FU MANCHU*

Before he left, he certified me with stamped papers. When I bring them to the office downtown, in return I'll pick up food-stamps, coupons, and then my rent will be taken care of. Later though…I was still too sore to move from the porch.

The clouds have tired of rain. The sky was a white candle color. I couldn't help noticing Albert's house across from me. It needed illumination. Who knows how they do it, but it always looks dark, as if no one is there. Once their curtains close, there are no lights, nor any sight of them.

Does a sort of Dr. Fu Manchu cavern hide in layers and tunnels under their house? Who knows what's going on in there? All I could see was their cat in the upstairs window, looking out, watching a strike of robins fly to my tree.

a Panama freighter

32. *OR I COULD GO*

I was drowsy enough to slip into sleep any minute when Pat Hatter's green spotted car swerved up to the curb. It had tarps roped over some big load that sunk the car low. It docked like a Panama freighter.

I gathered my shawls tightly around me.

Pat saw me and waved. He slowly came up to the wooden steps of the porch and said, "I need your help in a little adventure. All you have to do is be look-out. I know that's your specialty."

My arms hugged me. I could either sit here on the porch and watch how everything revolved on a sundial in search of the sun, or I could go follow Pat Hatter.

his way to the roof

33. *IN THE DIZZY HEIGHT*

I stood in a cold parking lot. Somewhere inside the wall of the Herald, Pat made his way to the roof. That was the plan anyway. He had a business card from KGUS, so he was allowed access to the radio antenna up there.

Some pigeons flicked about on a ledge, ten or twelve stories up, carrying on with their lives in the dizzy height.

Pat told me the parking lot was the best place for me to watch, where the metal fire escape let down and the water spout funnel dripped green. Meanwhile, the tarp covered thing stood waiting with me.

I heard a whistle in the distant air above me. Smaller than the wings of pigeons, I saw Pat waving his arms. He leaned over the edge like a spider at the top, lowering a wire.

34. *DISGUISE*

What we were doing was probably illegal. I could have been worried that someone would catch us, or at least ask who we were, but I was wearing my disguise. Blue overalls with my hair tucked in my cap. It's amazing what you can carry out when it looks like you're just another part of the anthill.

When we were finished, Pat Hatter's car returned me home. We were quiet on the ride. We were just lights on the road.

Pat stopped beside my yard and after I got out, his car hurried away, sticking to shadows.

The Herald building was clearly visible, red letters glowing on top. Pat Hatter's O was up there. He had taken down the E and moved the A over. HERALD became HAROLD. I couldn't help laughing.

Then I wondered what Albert would think.

35. *THE REELS OF SUPER-8*

I thought I would go out later to see the sign again when the stars were shining. There was always a chance that the Northern Lights would swerve around the sky too, like the ghostly spotlights over a used-car lot.

Candles lit the kitchen. I read from Emily Dickinson's thick cookbook of poems on the wooden counter. I followed her words. Cups of flour, butter, yeast, milk and honey, and soon the bread was baking. Three loaves would take a while, which left me time to do something I had been waiting for.

I went into the other room to see if Albert Jacks really existed in the reels of Super-8 film.

36. ALBERT'S REFLECTION

Albert's car faded in. It drove down the hill and parked in its usual spot beside the big cardboard box. I watched as he left the car smoking, while he hopped out and took the walk into his house.

Soon the front door swung open and Albert returned. He came out backwards, motioning his arms, urging something else out. "Come on!" he called, stopping by the wilted begonias. He was happy and eager and chirped encouragement, "Come on! This is going to be great!"

His wife stood in the doorway with another Albert Jacks. Albert's reflection mirrored and tilted until he slid out of the house. He moved away awkwardly down the steps, brushing against the flowers in a stiff-legged walk.

"That's good!" Albert beamed. "He can walk!" Albert told his wife, "He'll loosen up soon. Isn't this great? This is great, right? I won't have to go to work anymore! He can do it for me. We can—"

Albert quickly grabbed his double by the arm, led him out of the flower garden, and directed him back onto the cement. "That's okay, you're doing great. The car's right over here. Just follow the road. It will take you to the Herald."

The other Albert paused as Albert continued, "That's why I ordered you. So you can go to work in my place and free me up to be with my family." He clapped his twin on the shoulder. "You'll love my job!"

Albert's double didn't look so sure…The wheels were spinning…thinking it through. Suddenly, it broke free and staggered like Frankenstein back to the big cardboard box it arrived in.

37. *ABOVE THE ROOFTOPS*

While I was rewinding the film, I heard a wail from outside, across the street. I stopped the projector. I ran over to the door.

The long willow branches made a stain-glass weir over the picture of the blue neighborhood. I hopped down the steps in the dark yard of dropped leaves and branches. Above me were a couple of stars or satellites in the sky along with the moon and HAROLD.

Albert's door was open and framed his silhouette with yellow light. He stood on the grass wearing a robe, his arms held up and out like a Bedouin beholding the red glow above the rooftops.

38. *THE RED CROWN*

He talked loudly to his hand, holding onto one of those cell telephones people belong to now. "I can't believe it!" he bellowed. "No, I don't know anything about it, why would I?!" He let his other arm drop to tighten his bathrobe belt. "I don't know. I don't know…Yeah, I guess we'll just have to wait until tomorrow…I can't believe it!" he repeated as he started back across the lawn for the comfort of the warm curtained windows. He muttered something else before he closed the door.

But it was alright. Couldn't he see the joke? The red crown above town still laughed and burned like a comet in the heights.

39. *A TIME LIKE THIS*

I woke early. The white sky of the new winter day held like fresh paper to the window beside me. I pulled the blankets down over my shoulders and looked outside at the distant, black forest hills, the spilled roofs and parked cars and yellow leaves all over things.

I remember a time like this before, on another perfect morning when I crumpled up all the due bills that had been mailed to me for months on end. I took them out to the piles of leaves in the front yard and I tossed them in. Telephone, gas heat, electricity, garbage, sewer and rent—they all went. Even though made of paper, they fit right in.

40. *NEW MEANING*

Twigs, leaves, buds of dried flowers steam in the clay teapot. My day is free. I can stand at the window mesmerized by the orange and yellow backyard while the trees drop their goldfish leaves.

Albert left a while ago. I heard his car door slam. The car made a racket and pulled off into the street towards the Harold. I was sure blue torches and arc welders were all over the roof now, tearing the letters, but for one night at least there was new meaning for everyone.

The silver toaster popped up bread. I opened the cupboard to get a plate and the lidded glass jar of blackberry spread.

41. *WINDMILL*

Suzy Rake arrived at the laundromat as I was pulling my warm, soft tumbled clothes from the big round dryer. I tried to ignore her, falling in, searching deep in the hot metal windmill for lost socks and whatever. But she saw me, I could sense her approach. As I stuffed the last clothes in my bag, it happened.

She tapped my shoulder, "Did you hear?"

"Oh," I said. "Hello."

"About the neighbors?"

"Yes?" I spoke as patiently as I could.

"They went to see the doctor." She got closer; I knew she would. She lived across the street from me, in the house to the right of Albert. She was the tabloid version of what I watched. "They got that thing done…test tubes, super-drugs. Modern technology…" Her whisper came out like a clarinet reed cracking, "They're having triplets!"

The washing machines and dryers breathed in surprise.

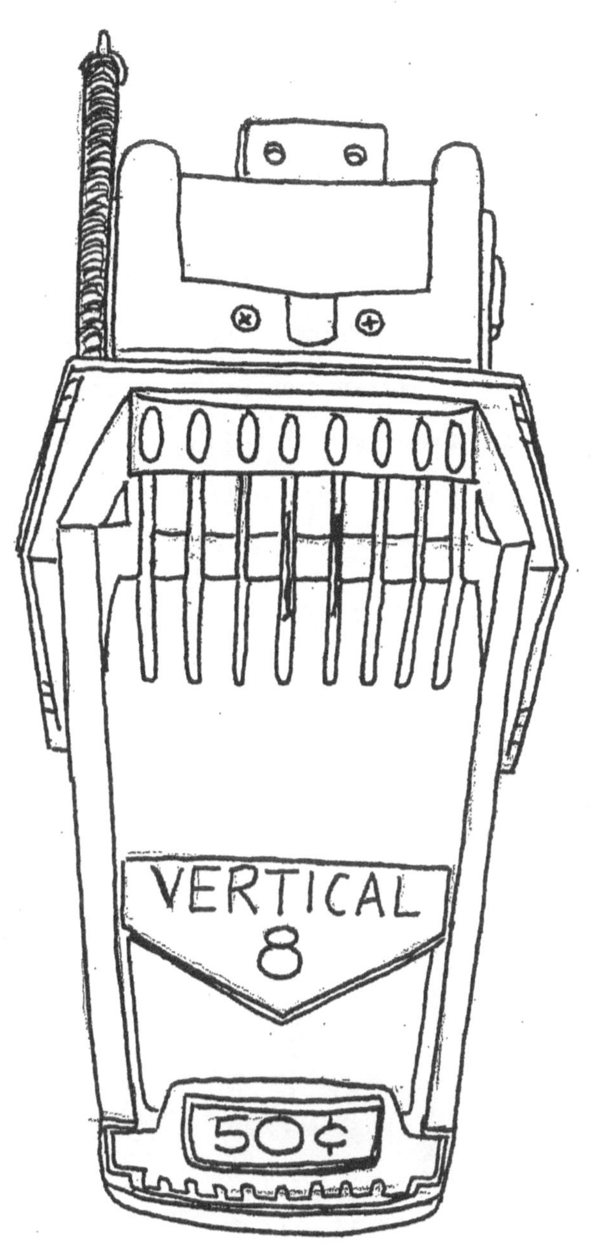

modern technology

42. *THE PAPER MACHINE*

I try to stay away from newspapers, but the headlines in the vending machine on the corner caught my attention.

City Searches for Missing E. There was a grainy photo of the Herald building roof with the letters on the sign spelling HAROLD. A destruction crew was trying to pull the word apart. They had already surrounded the A and the O.

I turned away from the paper machine. I still had a ways to go.

43. *SEEP*

I walked on leaves. The trees had lost most of their cover on the sky. A wet mist was drifting on green hills miles away.

Since I had to check on the painted stars, I decided to visit the King again. I crossed the street next to the park and stopped under the bridge.

My painting looked fine. Some water ran over it from the seep of the bridge.

I tracked into the low spread of ferns and rhododendron leaves, followed by a climb up a short hill. There was a telephone booth at the top.

cups and chopsticks

44. *IN THE STEAM*

After so many rings, Pat Hatter answered with the name of the kitchen, "Chang's Chinese Chow." He was in the middle of so many steel bowls to scrub, sending hours of plates, cups and chopsticks through the washing machine, while the calendar on the wall curled day after day in the steam.

Did he know they were looking for the E? I didn't dare ask him over the phone. You never know.

I told him it was me and to see me after work as soon as he could. He said he would. When we hung up, it was already reaching towards dark—time enough to run a movie while I waited.

45. *THE 10 FOOT E*

The 10 Foot E, swept in white title letters on black film, *Starring Pat Hatter.* Lightning cracked the sky above the city. A shadowy giant leaped from building to building. He jumped the canyon drops in between, carrying the Herald's E on his back. He went further, across tree branches, to the neighborhoods where he clung to the slanted tiles of a house.

When he stopped, he held to a television aerial and listened to distant police sirens. He peeled a big trap door from the roof, rested it open against the chimney and went down. Lightning above, he descended into eerie flashes of light inside the house.

The room below was a laboratory from the 1930s. Pat hurried over to his monstrous servant. "You did well," he said. He stuck the letter with electric wires, spinning lights and steam.

"Time is short," Pat said urgently, "we must give it life..." as the picture ended, curled and flapped.

46. PAT HATTER'S RETURN

Pat Hatter's return was in yellow headlights, a sawing engine and tires that cuffed up against the curb beside Albert's car. The sound stopped. Then I heard him crack the heavy metal door open.

I glanced out the window and saw the pearly lights strung on my porch. I poured hot water from the stove into the teapot and watched the current stir like leaves in the breeze.

Pat's feet clomped to the door and I let him inside. A cold night balloon fell in with him too, gusting to the rafters.

"Brrr," I said.

"What am I going to do?" he burst. "I have that ten foot letter E the whole city is looking for!" He dropped into a chair like a cannonball into sand.

47. A FOSSIL

I turned the window curtain aside with the curl of my finger to peek at his car out there. There wasn't a letter on the rooftop, covered by tarps. "So…where did you hide it?"

He rubbed his hands over his knees. "Somewhere they'll never find it. I hope. It's just that, when you do something like this, there's always a fear of what if—? Some kid might be playing around being a pirate…or the mailman notices that something big was dragged across your lawn…" He threw his hands in the air hopelessly. "Who knows? It's too late now anyway. Even a fossil gets found sooner or later."

"Where did you hide it, Pat?"

He pointed slowly to my floor, "Down there."

48. *A MUMMY*

We followed the trail of it across the lawn. The heavy letter had been pulled very early this morning, under the leaves of my willow. It left rubbled leaves piled to the right side of my house then it crushed a path towards the two wooden storm doors that led into my cellar.

"Pat…" I worried as I pulled open the door. I found the light bulb string. Sure enough, further off, washed over with cobwebs, there hid the big letter E. It was leaning on flattened stale cardboard.

"Nobody saw," he assured me. "I had it wrapped up like a mummy when I dragged it in here."

I shut my eyes heavily and sighed, then opened them wide—to crunching leaves approaching and suddenly a flashlight found us there.

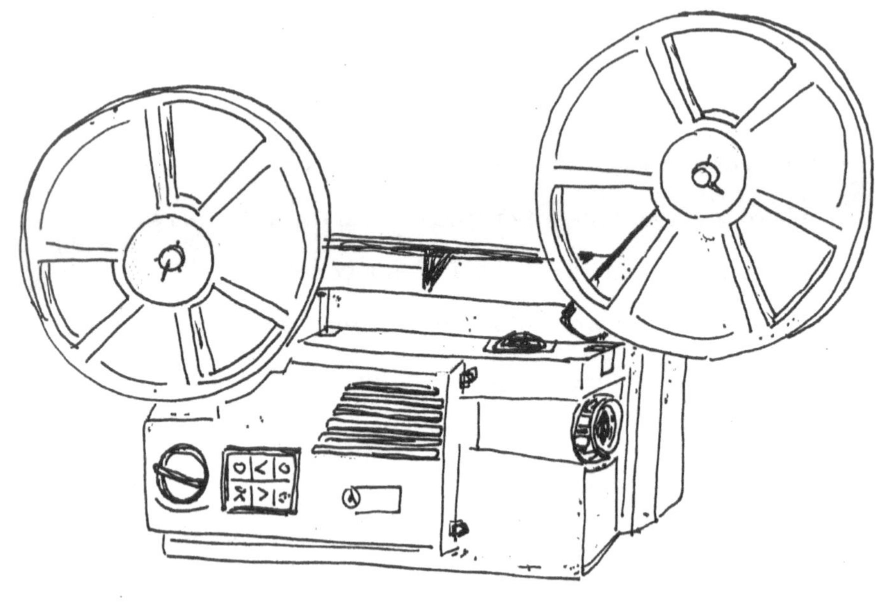

"I've been watching you"

49. *THIS ANGEL*

The silhouette planted in front of us fanned a flashlight into the open cellar door, laughing and turning off the beam. A familiar voice said, "I've been watching you…I figured it was you who took that E from the tower. Funny, I don't know how I knew…"

In the dark with us, my eyes adjusting to see, illumined by the moody colors of the church's stain-glass next door, stood Albert Jacks.

"Are you a cop?" stammered Pat.

Albert laughed, "No, I'm not a cop. Relax, everything's fine. In fact I'd like to help you out if I can. I'd be interested in taking that E off your hands." He stepped closer to us and lowered his voice, "See, I have a plan for it."

Who would have thought Albert would save the day? Pat and I just stared at him. I always had a feeling we would meet, but it would still take a moment for this angel to register, like an image in the wash of a photography darkroom.

50. *ANOTHER MIRACLE*

It was another miracle that nobody noticed us in the midnight, pulling that E out of the cellar, across the street, and finally around the back of Albert's house.

He had a shed amid the frozen branches of dried herbs and flowers. We got the letter in there alright and locked the door when we left.

While resting, catching our breath and puffing at the starry sky, Albert told me, "I live across the street from you and I wonder all the time what the holy heck you're up to. Tell me—" he pointed over the blunt points of roofs in the direction of the newspaper, "Did you make that O?"

I had never been this close to him before. It was strange in a way; he didn't look the same as in his movies. I would hate to think I was wrong about him. I looked away. "Pat made it," I said shyly.

Albert turned to him, "I have a new job for you, Pat. That is, if you're interested."

51. *YOU WILL SEE*

Later that night, as Pat and I were unwinding, the newspaper building surprised us with a joke of its own. The partly dismantled faulty red lights floating on top flashed continuosly HAR…HAR…HAR…Pat thought that was even better than what we had done.

I asked Pat about his commission and he just smiled, promising me, "You will see…" He worked for Albert in great secrecy.

What a relief. I could watch this dream like a movie taking care of itself. Time and I sat together happily on the porch, watching through the willow as the sun, moon, clouds and clear sky passed and the cold world turned back into warm.

It took Pat Hatter months, curving, turning and smoothing the letter E. The summer was here. It was the night the triplets were born before the whole neighborhood found out what he made.

52. *3*

Unveiled for the triplets their first night here on Earth, glowing in red neon beauty above the dark green eaves of Albert's roof was a ten foot number 3. Fortunately, nobody ever noticed the resemblance to the Herald's E.

Since then, it has become one of the sights of the evening city, the sort of thing that draws people to stop and stare like moths.

Below, in the light of their warm living room, the Jacks family gathers at their window for bows. They don't seem to mind being stars.

And it's still a thrill to watch them perform from my home across the street. Every evening I can see their little movie play until Albert Jacks finally waves and pulls the curtain goodnight.

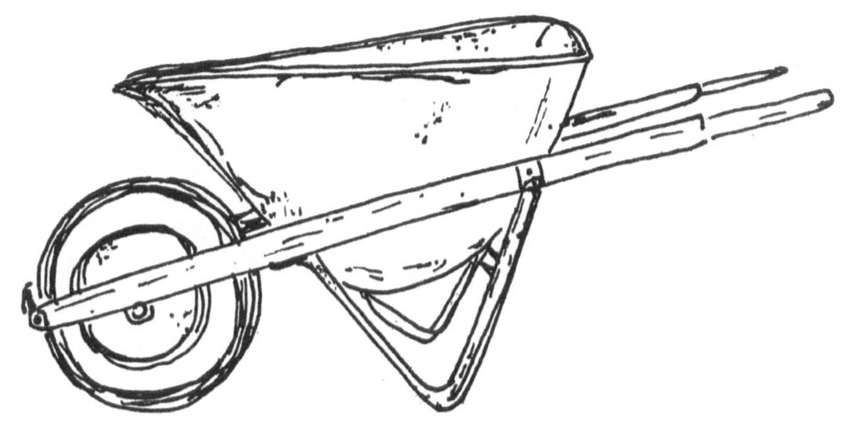

LEMONADE

17¢
so much
the current
radish
in the air
the radiator
clara
delight
the 10 penny wonder show
example
a shadow
soaked
spilled
the shroud
safe from the war
the doves
believing
in a cloud
into the fog
over and over
asleep
chickens

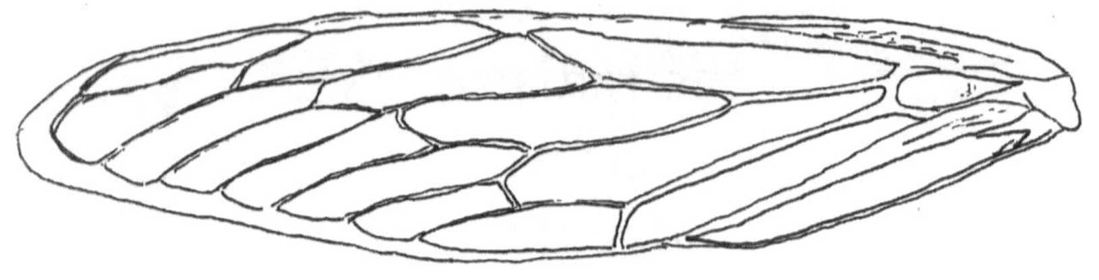

frail as cellophane

17¢

I only have 17¢ to put on the letter. I feed the silver and copper change into the stamp meter and it gives me a little pair of wings to stick on the envelope.

They look frail as cellophane. They shiver and weakly lift the letter out of my hands. I guess I didn't put enough money on, but that's all I have.

I watch the letter step up into the breeze above the sidewalk and for a moment it gets lost against the gray bricks of the freight building. Then I see it plainly, hover against a blue patch of sky, just before it falls.

so much

So much depends on knowing the answer to the unknowable things—the small mysteries that end up ruling our day to day life, like how many stamps go on a letter and how far will it fly on 17¢? I didn't know until I found out.

The answer is not quite a full city block. And if it's lucky, with the lift of the breeze, another seven foot distance at the most. I find the letter resting against an electric horse hitch and I pick it up sourly.

If I have felt anything lately, it is sourness. Not for what I'm doing, what I'm doing is okay, but for how I'm paid for doing it. I'm being paid to translate old black and white motion. And I'm being paid in lemonade. You might wonder how that's going to help me survive.

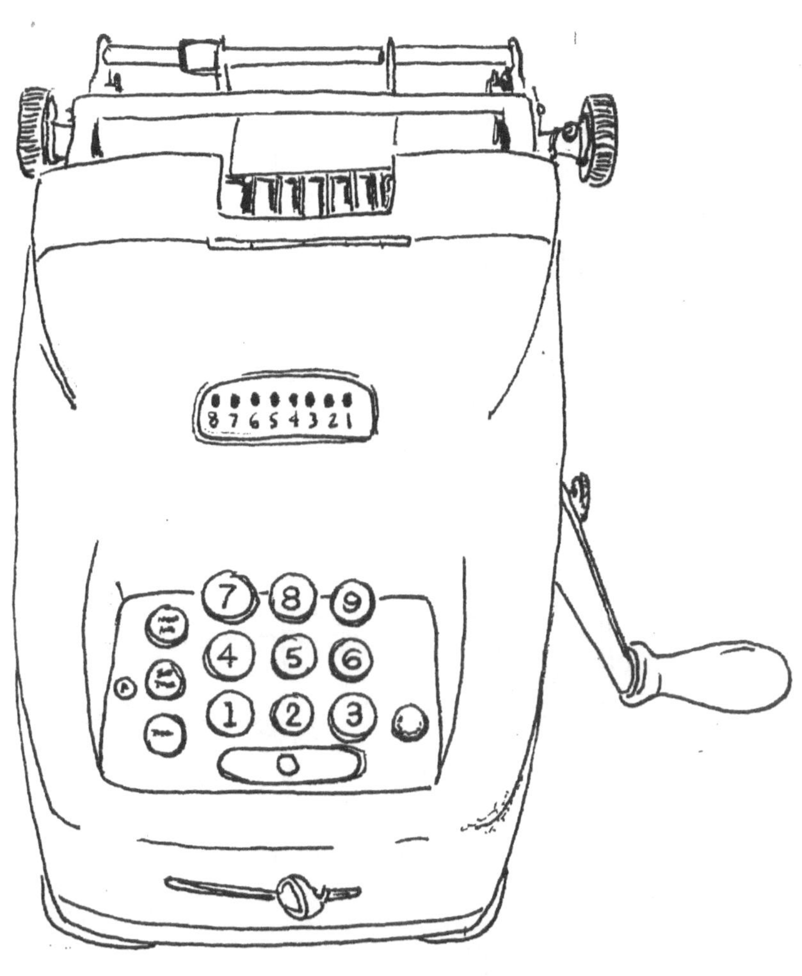

knowing the answer

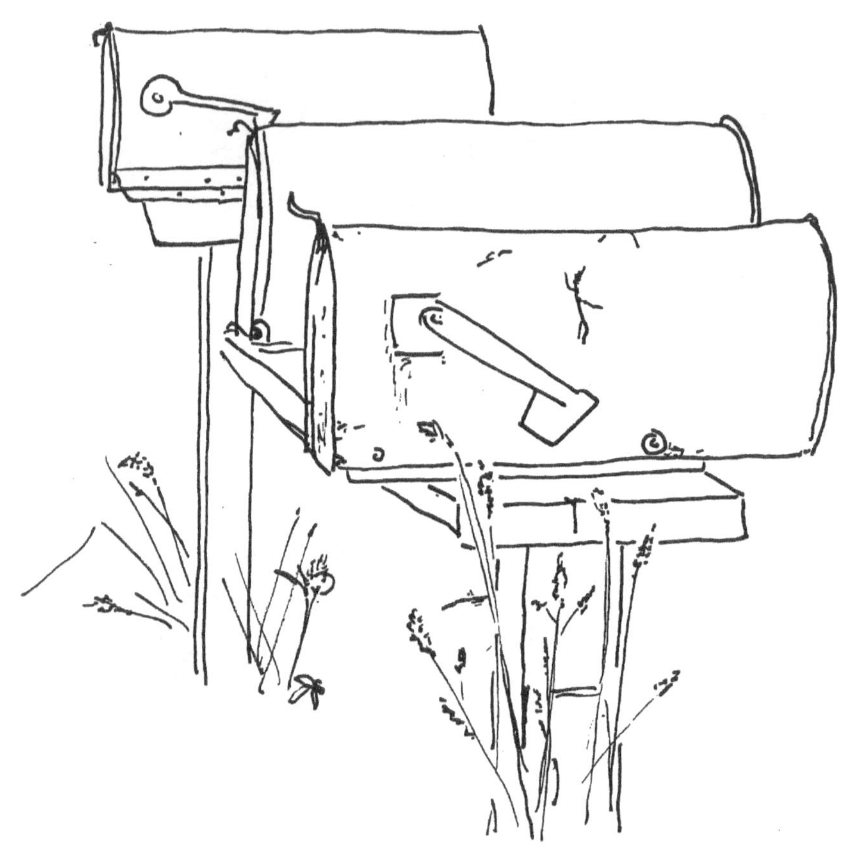

cages full of doves

the current

I take the letter back to my apartment building. I can
revive it. I'm not worried. I have an idea to get it further than
it went before.

After all the traffic on the way, thinking about things,
the white chickens get out of my shadow before the stairwell
and up I climb. There aren't any windows but the blue
wartime emergency lights glow and crackle on the walls. Each
step makes me feel like a walking x-ray.

I'm always glad to get out of there, where the steps
run out onto the roof of the building into the clear air,
barrage balloons and the cold weather of early winter.
Wooden and wire cages full of doves watch me. I move
towards the poplar trees reaching their leafless branches up
over the edge of the apartment building.

A breeze could easily take hold of the letter and carry
it for miles in the current over the city. I touch the wings.
They are rested and ready to try again.

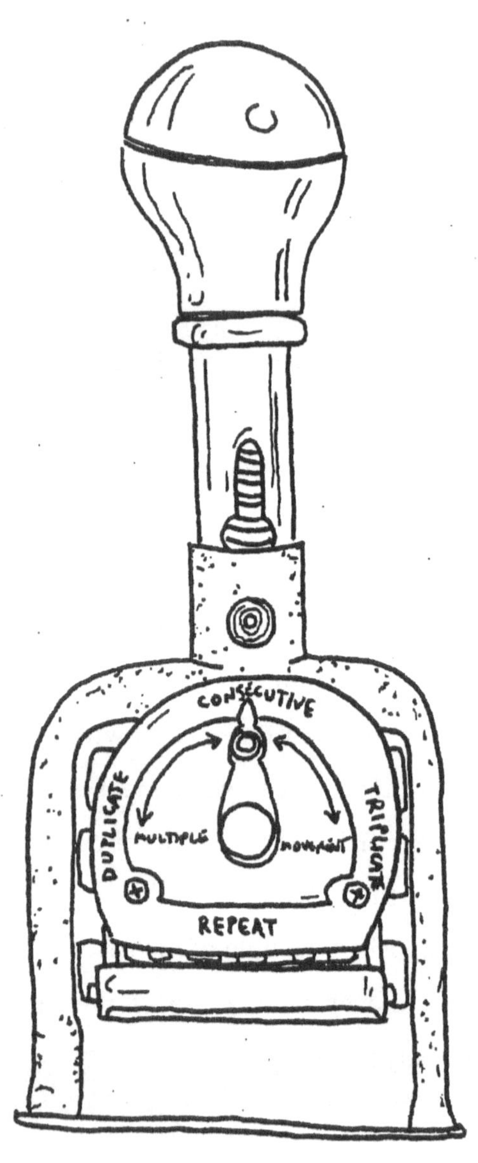

the same lesson

radish

Upon a red fire-escape, I lean. The city is decorated for another war. It's been going on for a while. It's sad, for all of human history they have to keep learning the same lesson over and over again. There are flags everywhere and those swollen balloons roped to the neighborhood chimneys. The balloon above this building makes a round shadow over half our roof.

I hold the letter out at arm's length and just as I am about to let it go, a voice calls my last name.

"Radish!"

I return the letter to my pocket before I turn around.

I know what I will see. I can hear the scrape of its little legs as it approaches.

"Radish, what are you doing up here?"

"I'm trying to mail you the script additions."

My alarm clock has crawled all this way up to the roof to find me. There is no getting away. It wobbles and glints, a copper grin across its face. The long silver antenna trailing out of it is connected to my boss, the Hollywood mogul, Peter Simon. That is his voice speaking through my clock, tracking me, telling me, "Just read me what you've got, Radish."

I start to open the envelope.

"Naww. Let's go to the apartment first. It's safer. Give me a lift." The contraption squawks and rocks on its pins.

I carry my boss in the alarm clock back down the stairs.

in the air

My room is a lemon. It's in the air…the bed in the corner, the bookshelf, the table with paper and pens, dictionary and movie projector, the window light above the stove, the radiator that steams…everything floats as if in the same amber that catches you too the second the door opens. The faint whirr is the radiator turning lemonade into a yellow glow everywhere.

"Okay, read me what you got," the alarm clock directs.

I set him on a corner of the table and start to open the letter, pressing my finger into the paper corner to tear it when he interrupts me suddenly, "Wait a second…What's that?"

Peter Simon is listening to someone miles away who I can't see. I just stare at the clock of him. "Oh…Okay," he grumbles. "Listen, Radish. Don't do anything with that letter yet. I have to go now."

Then the alarm clock gets quiet, or rather, returns to its ticking. It is a machine, but I have to be ready. At any second it can turn back into him.

the radiator

Lemonade didn't seem like such a bad thing at first. Cartons of lemonade started arriving soon after I accepted Peter Simon's offer to rewrite the old French movie. They needed a poet to translate. I said sure, why not, because at that time I had nothing and the future was pressing on a thin leaning wall. Lemonade seemed good. But after the kitchen was filled with stacked boxes of the stuff, I realized I had to do something with them. So this is what I figured out...

I grab a box off the stack and walk over to the radiator. I pour it in those metal ribs and the radiator sighs contentment. Anything has energy in it. I discovered it in the yellow pulp and sugar and now everything in my room runs on lemonade.

anything has energy

Clara

"Barrow!"

I look out the window and see who is calling my name. I wave at Clara. She has pushed her red wheelbarrow full of vegetables to the curbside and is reeling me down.

I know she is on her way to the 10 Penny Wonder Show. Lately we've been going together. I don't know…I hope she knows…I hope she knows she's my dream.

I grab a carton of lemonade and leave my warm room and especially the clock with its sleeping tick.

delight

After I poured the lemonade into the red wheelbarrow tank, I got onto the edge with her and held on as we drove out onto the cobblestones.

Clara is my delight. As soon as I'm done with this Hollywood thing, I'm taking her far away from this war. I've been thinking about islands. The ones that sit in light blue water. Palms and fruit and pleasing sunshine...As soon as I know the right one, I'll take her there.

She drives the red wheelbarrow like a little land boat, turning the tiller and sending us under the arches of the aqueduct. We follow in the blue shadow racing beside the pillars that hold it up. If all the shaking winter kale and cabbage we sit on can keep from flying off, I can too.

the 10 penny wonder show

Clara pulls us in the space between two parked Model T 2s. People near us stop and look at the smell of lemon next to them. I wave. I always feel like some sort of star when I'm with Clara. The world seems happy to obey the laws of the movies as we drop to the cobblestones and push a red wheelbarrow into the crowd of colors, talk and music.

We are in the middle of the 10 Penny Wonder Show. You can imagine us. You may have been there before. It's a dream that it's even here at all.

example

Clara and I set up the vegetables she grows. Of course I've talked to her about growing lemons. She's thinking about it; I'm showing her how they can change the world. I hope we can. We could set an example for everyone. No more going into another war over energy. They could stop their war plans and start planting instead. There could be lemon trees spread out in windmill orchards and on every corner waiting if you need to plug in. A dream could all begin with Clara and me.

I can see it happening, but I live in a different kind of world.

By the time I leave that daydream, Clara has her garden in rows on the table top.

the shadow unzips

a shadow

Glazed with rain, water makes diamonds on everything. We have the afternoon to sit here together. A little clay charcoal stove pours out heat beside our feet. We are watching an old man reading poetry in the ivy when it hits.

A shadow drops over the table and a voice orders, "Let's see your flags!" The rest of the shadow unzips to reveal the soldier underneath that camouflage. The shadow is half open like a corn husk to let the soldier reach out. "Flags!"

Clara moves before I can. She has more experience with this I guess. I just freeze looking at the man with the gun.

Clara takes out a flag and, "Oh—" she pulls out another flag too. "This one is his. I'm holding it for him, his pockets are filled with holes."

"You better find a way to carry that flag on you," the soldier warns me. "It's the law. You don't want me to catch you without it." Then he buckles himself back into his shadow.

I try to keep my eye on him, but he seems to vanish into the air.

soaked

It wasn't long after that when it really began to rain, a cold rain that reminds you it is winter. The fair folded itself up like a flower in the storm. We put our things back busily.

Luckily, I found a big yellow square of cloth on the pavement and I held it over Clara while we rode away on the red wheelbarrow.

The road was dented with full puddles. We seemed to hit every one. Once we were soaked, the shroud didn't matter anymore. I shoved the flap into my coat pocket and held onto the wagon edges while we flew along.

The little front wheel threw a spray outwards on either side of us. Sometimes we ducked behind the waterfalls spilling off the aqueduct.

When we come out of the shadows again, wheels rumbling through the dark city, we see fog has walked feet all over the town.

spilled

Water is on everything as I open the window of my apartment to wave goodbye to Clara. I see her down on the shiny pavement.

She pushes the red wheelbarrow off the curb, across the street. It is getting darker and she has turned on the lights along the wheelbarrow. It looks like she is pushing a Christmas tree in the rain.

Anyway, I am wet and freezing and I have to pour more lemonade in the radiator to get this place warm again.

I take a box off the yellow pyramid and I open it beside the radiator. My hands are so cold I spilled some on the floor. I use the shroud from my pocket to sop it up then I stretch that fairground cloth, damp with rainwater and lemonade, out over the hissing steam of the radiator.

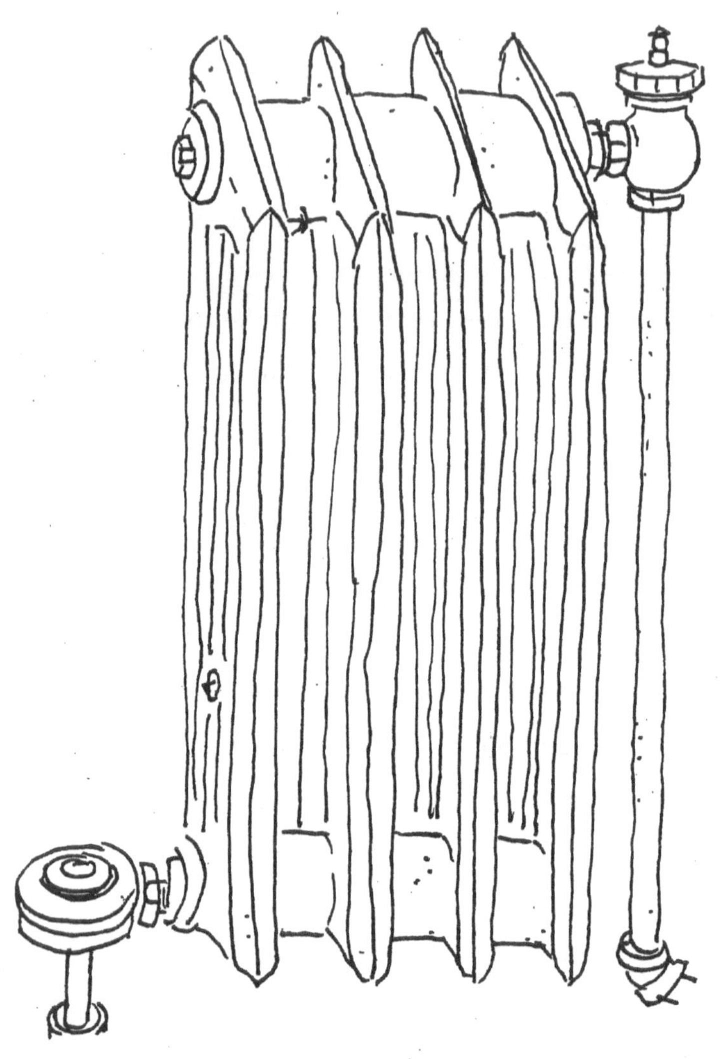

a cloud looking out

the shroud

I don't move from the radiator. I need to dry out too. I feel like a cloud looking out the window at the weather. The glass panel shakes with gusts of wind.

Getting warm, rubbing my hands together over the heat, I notice a strange change in the cloth draped over it.

As the wet leaves it, a face is forming in the threads.

I watch long enough to notice there are eyes staring at me.

I keep watching more appear. It takes a few minutes of the hushing steam and then, there it is complete. After all that time watching the transformation, I am not surprised when the shroud talks.

safe from the war

"The war," it croaks. The effort makes it wave. "I have to warn you about the war."

"I know," I agree. "The world is in trouble." We have crazy leaders who are giving us nightmares. The days are stacked up like railway cars in a slow motion crash.

"No. You don't know. I can see something waiting to happen. That's why I'm here—to make sure you and Clara are safe from the war."

"Clara and me?"

"Of course," the shroud says urgently. "There's little time. She needs to be with you. It will happen tonight."

"Okay, okay."

"You have to send for her."

"I will. I'm just trying to think..." Finally, I see us escaping to that tropical island. But how? "Can we tie ourselves to a balloon?"

The shroud stares at me impatiently.

I say, "I'll send her a letter." I tear open the Hollywood envelope. I take the film script out and sit down to write Clara instead.

I stare at the white paper. "What should I say though? Should I run away with her? Where should we go? Where in the world is safe?"

"There's no time for that." The shroud's eyes roam past me. "You'll be safe in this room. The lemonade will protect you. That's why I made sure you would have plenty of it."

"*You* made sure?" I stare at the face. "*You've* been sending me the lemonade?"

"Yes. Just make sure the air in here is filled with lemonade steam."

"So all this time I've been working for nothing..." I mumble.

"No, *this* is something! Hurry!"

I look at the paper and remember. "I know! I can invite her to see the movie! I always wanted her to...I'm kind of doing it for her."

the doves

When I am up on the roof again, I wake the doves. They wash about in their cages as I come out of the stairway, catching them with green light and footsteps. Try as I might to walk peacefully on my way, it's no use. Every bird is watching me.

"Sorry, I'm just..." I try to explain to them. I like those doves. I don't want to scare them. We share the roof, my ceiling is their floor. At night, they coo me to sleep. And when they're out flying free, some will always land for a while on my window ledge.

My shadow creaks over the tar patched roof to the edge where I take out the letter. Searchlights sweep the sky, making stripes in the night, clouds run through like tigers.

Something does seem to be out there. It feels like more than a storm. The wind breathes and I wait for just the right moment to toss Clara's message. The wings that cost me 17¢ whirr again. It has to be enough. I hope more than ever.

believing

"So you're going to show her the movie?" the alarm clock startles me. Peter Simon's chalky voice continues as I enter my room, "Hey, maybe while you're at it you can finish the script!"

I don't listen to that chatter though. I was sending him his story in bits and pieces. I was giving him dreams. Sometimes all you have are fragments. That has to be enough.

I go over to the window so I can keep watch for Clara. I laugh at myself behaving this way, hoping she will read my message and hurry here, believing in what a shroud told me.

"Did your letter fly?" the shroud asks.

"It's in the sky."

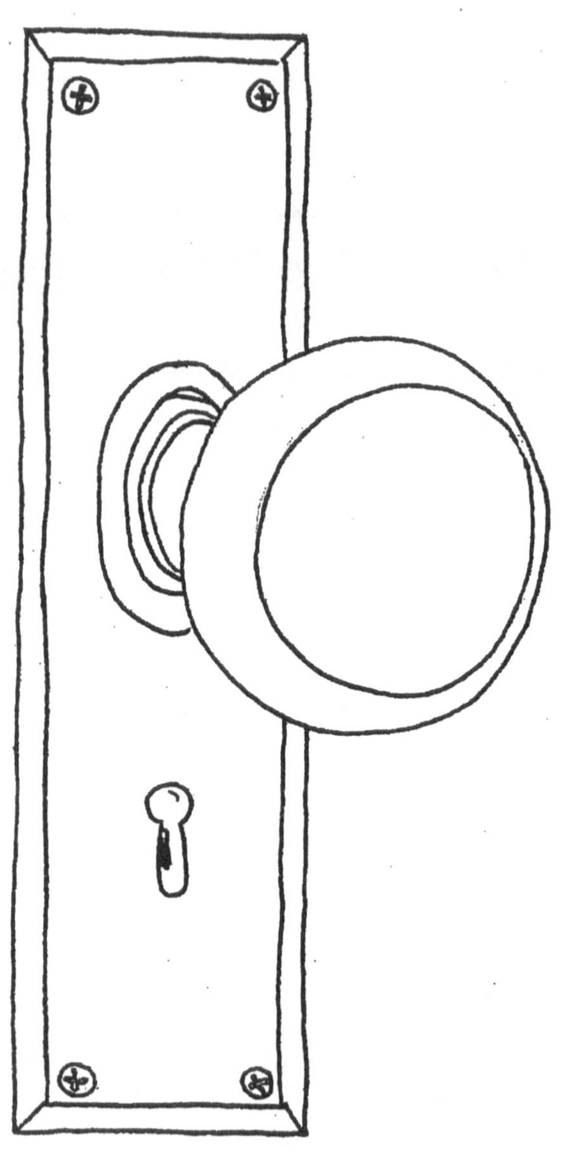

wait for her

in a cloud

While I wait for her to arrive, I listen to the shroud and the alarm clock. They talk back and forth with me in the middle until I leave the window.

I top off the radiator again, making sure it is full of lemonade. The shroud keeps telling me how important the lemonade steam is. I even have pans full of lemonade cooking on the stove. The air is thick as fog when the door starts to knock.

"She's here!" the alarm clock caws.

"Finally!" says the shroud.

Before I open the door though, I want them to know something. They are driving me up the wall. "Listen you two, you've got to be peaceful and quiet and stay out of this now. I want her to feel at home."

Miraculously, they hush and then, when I open the door, the steam rushes out around Clara, capturing her in a cloud.

into the fog

"Is your room always like this?" Clara asks me. How can I tell her about the lemonade and the alarm clock and the shroud? I show her through the cloud to a soft place on the couch. From the kitchen, she looks like a spirit in the other room.

Pouring more lemonade into pans on the oven, I say. "No, no. There's something wrong with the radiator."

She laughs. "I hope we can see the movie."

"Don't worry," I assure her. I leave the kitchen and walk towards her shape.

The projector stands in a swirl. It is all prepared with the first reel threaded on.

"I've been waiting forever to show you this film."

"I know. Thanks for your invitation." She sat beside the white envelope with the tired wings. "Come sit with me, Barrow."

"I will, I will. Let me put on this record first. The soundtrack stopped working so I play it with music." I tip the vinyl circle out of its sleeve. "Well, I hope you like it, Clara."

I let the Schumann piano quintet crackle and the movie light reach out into the fog.

a spirit in the other room

over and over

I sit beside Clara. The spent wings of the 17¢ stamp have since turned to dust, but they brought her here.

We watch the movie I've seen so many times over and over before. I want to tell her everything. "This is from 1937. It was just before their war began. It wasn't so different or so far away from us. It never really is. The people go back and forth on the streets but you can tell something is going to happen…then it did."

asleep

With her I forget about the rest of the world until the shroud rustles on the radiator. "I'll be right back," I promise Clara and leave the sofa.

I feel like a fool leaving her for a radiator. I listen beside it. The shroud whispers, "I want you to know I'm taking care of you. Soon you will both seem to fall asleep. Don't worry though. You'll be protected. When you wake up the war will be over."

Outside, the dark silhouettes of the town show against the flying rain and wind. As I watch, the sky fills with every little scrap of paper or cloth whatnot called to rattle and scurry over the window, sealing us tight.

The heat lifts the shroud off the radiator and it floats to the window sill, where it spreads itself flat as a blanket across the glass.

I find Clara again and it is like the shroud promised. We are asleep before I know.

chickens

A big yellow sun wakes us up. It glows on the covered window. We are warm. The room is still until Clara stretches, brushes her arm across me. "What happened?"

"It's morning!" I laugh. I feel floating. We have been together all this time.

There is an unpeeling sound as the shroud falls off the window, onto the floor like a dry leaf.

"Where's the movie?" Clara yawns and smiles, "I think I fell asleep during it."

"So did I!" I get up. I have to see what happened outside. The window is stickered but I can see daylight let through where the shroud had been.

The storm is over. Empire litter fills the branches, making bright leaves on the trees. I see birds in them, singing.

I can't tell…Maybe the world has been through a war, but it looks okay now.

I put my hand on the flat warm glass. Some dew pebbled the rough brick sill. Dropping off to the street, I can see the new morning light on Clara's parked red wheelbarrow and down around the poplar trunk, gathered around the tidal pools, are the same white chickens.

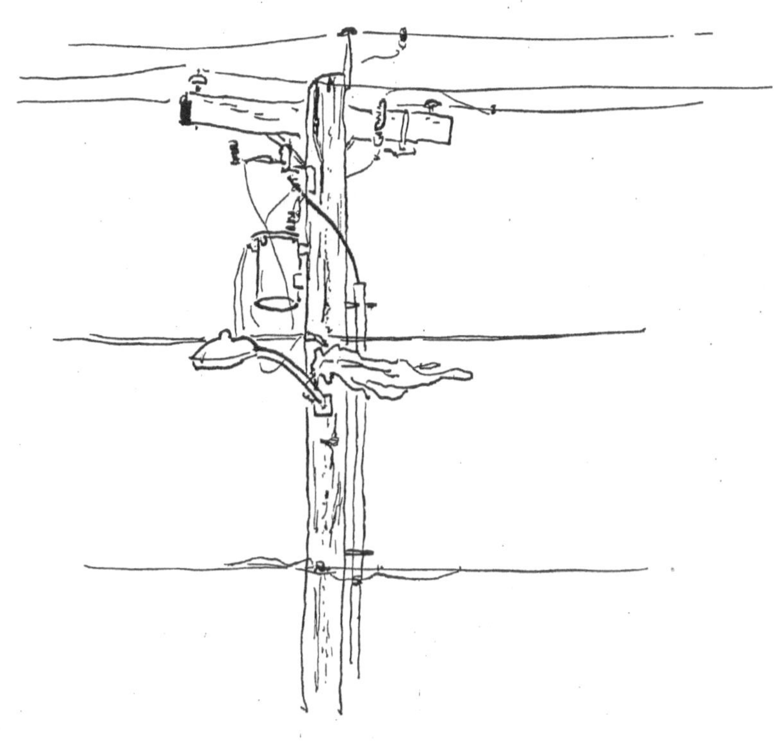

empire litter

Other Books by the Author

Ohio Trio (Bottom Dog Press 2001)

Bowl of Water (Bottom Dog Press 2003)

Another Life (Bird Dog Publishing 2007)

Home Recordings (Bird Dog Publishing 2009)

The Mermaid Translation (Bird Dog Publishing 2010)

The Selected Correspondence of Kenneth Patchen

    edited by Allen Frost (Bottom Dog Press 2012)

The Wonderful Stupid Man (Bird Dog Publishing 2012)